DAVE HUGHES & HOLLY IFE

Illustrated by **Philip Bunting**

To Maximilien, Sidney, Zelda, Célestine, Walter, Audrey and all the other little people in our life who love books—D.H. & H.I.

For Santa (you know who you are)—P.B.

First published in 2018 by Scholastic Press
An imprint of Scholastic Australia Pty Limited

First published in the UK in 2020 by Scholastic Children's Books
Euston House, 24 Eversholt Street
London, NW1 1DB
A division of Scholastic Ltd
www.scholastic.co.uk

London – New York – Toronto – Sydney – Auckland
Mexico City – New Delhi – Hong Kong

ISBN 978 0702 30547 4

Printed in China

1 3 5 7 9 10 8 6 4 2

Typeset in Argone LC Light.

Martha May had marvellous manners,
especially at Christmas.

She wrote beautiful Christmas cards to her friends.

She helped choose thoughtful gifts for her family.

She even pretended to enjoy Great-Aunt Edith's famous Christmas pudding.

On Christmas Eve, just before bed,
Martha May used her best handwriting
to write a thank-you card to Santa Claus.

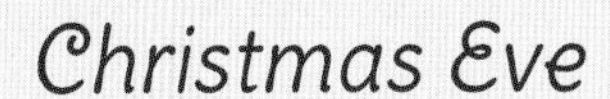

Christmas Eve

Dear Santa,

Thank you for my present,
I'm sure I'll love it, even
if it's more woolly socks.

Love,
Martha May

Martha May left the card next to some gingerbread for Santa, and put carrots out for the reindeer.

She said goodnight to her parents and went to bed.

Martha May was fast asleep until she was woken up by the sound of very loud, and very impolite, eating.

CRUNCH.
CRUNCH.
CRUNCH.

CRUNCH.
CRUNCH.
CRUNCH.

Martha May crept out of her room.
And there, in her kitchen, was . . .

SANTA!

Hello, young lady—you're supposed to be asleep!

Sorry, Santa, I was asleep, but your munching and crunching woke me up. Those carrots are supposed to be for the reindeer!

I know, but delivering presents makes me so hungry!

Martha May had marvellous manners and she did not want Santa to be hungry when he had so much work to do.

Would you like some of my Great-Aunt Edith's Christmas pudding?

she asked politely.

Well, maybe just one small slice.

Martha May cut a slice of pudding and Santa ate it.

Martha May decided not to tell him it was bad manners to talk with his mouth full.

Santa's tummy started to . . .
GURGLE!

'Would you like any more?' asked Martha May politely.

So Martha May cut another slice.

And another . . .

And another . . .

CRACK!

GURGLE!

GURGLE!

GURGLE!

GURGLE!

. . . until Santa Claus had eaten the WHOLE Christmas pudding!

'It's time for me to go,' Santa said.
'I hope you like your present tomorrow.
It's not woolly socks, by the way.'

Santa Claus stood up to leave.
His tummy **GURGLED** and **BULGED** under his red suit.

Santa took his place on his sleigh
and the reindeer started to pull . . .

but the sleigh didn't move.

Santa! What have you been eating?
You know you are only supposed to have one little treat at each house!
Now you're too heavy, Santa!
We're stuck! Christmas is ruined!

'Oh dear. What am I going to do?' said Santa. His tummy **GURGLED LOUDER** and **LOUDER**. Martha May had an idea.

She whispered in Santa's ear and he smiled. And then Santa let out the most SPECTACULAR, AMAZING, INCREDIBLE . . .

FAR

His fart sounded like **Jingle Bells**, it smelt like cinnamon and it sparkled like glitter.

Martha May watched as the sleigh whooshed across the night sky.
Houston . . .
Bvvvrrt!
And I thought
I was gaseous!
That's a bit
rude-olph you, Santa!
RATTLE!
Hissss!
As she got back into bed,
Martha May had three thoughts . . .
I will have to tell Great-Aunt Edith
how much Santa enjoyed her pudding.

Whoosh!
Bat out of smell!
Mmmm, cinnamon.
Puff!
HO HO HO!
Thank you, Martha May!
Her second thought was . . .
I wonder what my Christmas present is.

And just before she fell asleep,
she thought . . .

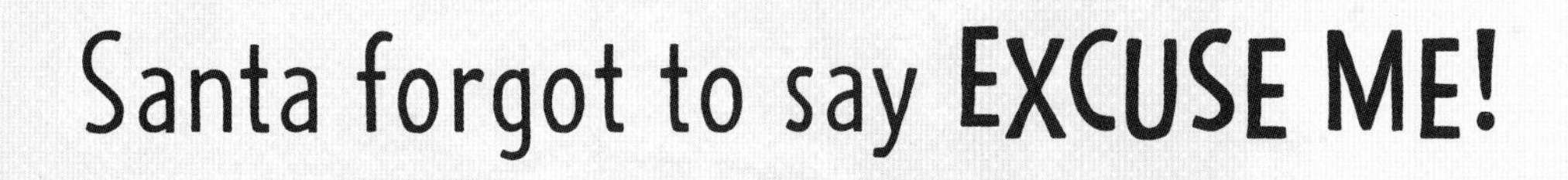
Santa forgot to say **EXCUSE ME!**

1001
extremely polite
FART
JOKES
By Prof. I. B. Windy
To Martha May,
From Santa.